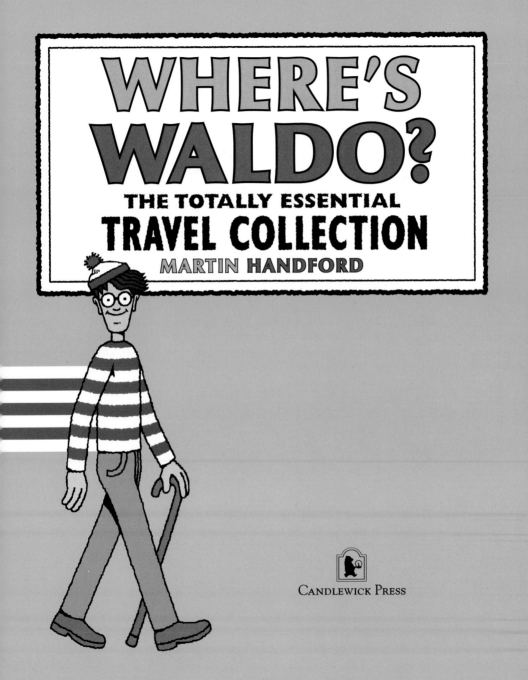

WHERE'S WALDO?

THE TOTALLY ESSENTIAL
TRAVEL COLLECTION

MARTIN HANDFORD

CANDLEWICK PRESS

HI, WALDO-WATCHERS!

ARE YOU READY TO JOIN ME ON MY SEVEN
FANTASTIC ADVENTURES?

- WHERE'S WALDO?
- WHERE'S WALDO NOW?
- WHERE'S WALDO? THE FANTASTIC JOURNEY
- WHERE'S WALDO? IN HOLLYWOOD
- WHERE'S WALDO? THE WONDER BOOK
- WHERE'S WALDO? THE GREAT PICTURE HUNT!
- WHERE'S WALDO? THE INCREDIBLE PAPER CHASE

CAN YOU FIND THE FIVE INTREPID TRAVELERS
AND THEIR PRECIOUS ITEMS IN EVERY SCENE?

ODLAW   WIZARD WHITEBEARD   WENDA   WOOF   WALDO

WALDO'S KEY   WOOF'S BONE   WENDA'S CAMERA

WIZARD WHITEBEARD'S SCROLL   ODLAW'S BINOCULARS

WAIT, THERE'S MORE! AT THE BEGINNING AND
END OF EACH ADVENTURE, FIND A FOLD-OUT
CHECKLIST WITH HUNDREDS MORE THINGS
TO LOOK FOR.

WOW! WHAT A SEARCH!

BON VOYAGE!

HI, FRIENDS!

MY NAME IS WALDO. I'M JUST SETTING OFF ON A WORLDWIDE HIKE. YOU CAN COME TOO. ALL YOU HAVE TO DO IS FIND ME.

I'VE GOT ALL I NEED—WALKING STICK, KETTLE, MALLET, CUP, BACKPACK, SLEEPING BAG, BINOCULARS, CAMERA, SNORKEL, BELT, BAG, AND SHOVEL.

I'M NOT TRAVELING ON MY OWN. WHEREVER I GO, THERE ARE LOTS OF OTHER CHARACTERS FOR YOU TO SPOT. FIRST FIND WOOF (BUT ALL YOU CAN SEE IS HIS TAIL), WENDA, WIZARD WHITEBEARD, AND ODLAW. THEN FIND 25 WALDO-WATCHERS SOMEWHERE, EACH OF WHOM APPEARS ONLY ONCE IN MY TRAVELS. CAN YOU FIND ONE OTHER CHARACTER WHO APPEARS IN EVERY SCENE? ALSO IN EVERY SCENE, CAN YOU SPOT MY KEY, WOOF'S BONE, WENDA'S CAMERA, WIZARD WHITEBEARD'S SCROLL, AND ODLAW'S BINOCULARS?

WOW! WHAT A SEARCH! Waldo

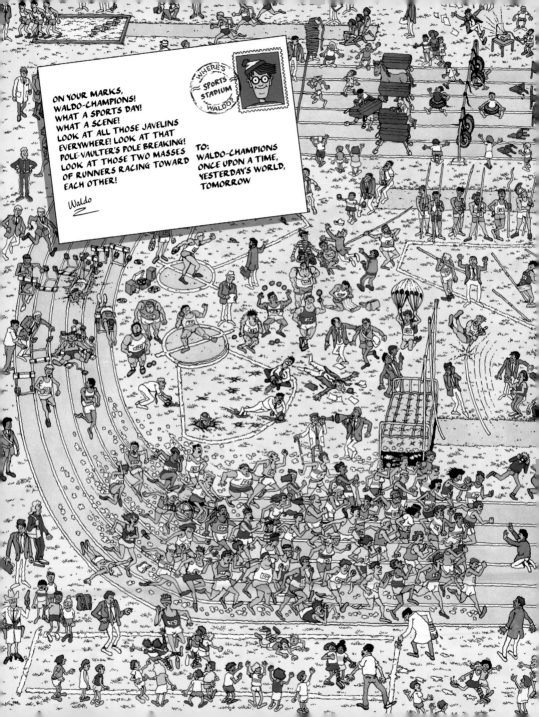

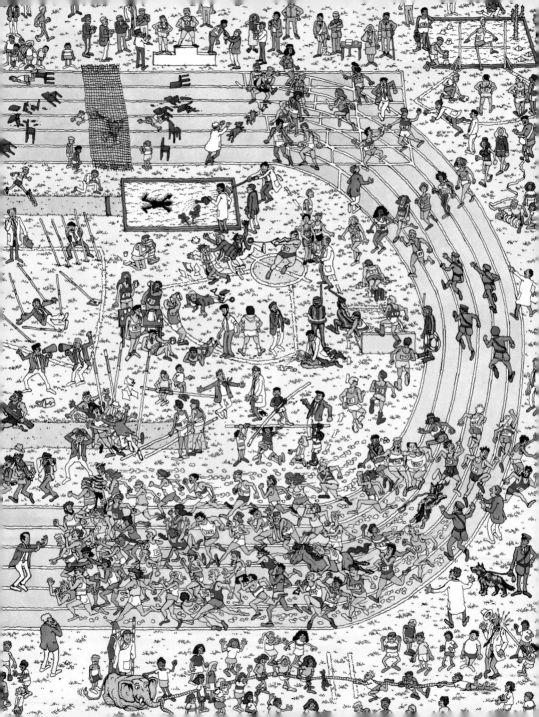

STEP RIGHT UP, WALDO-FUN LOVERS!
WOW! I'VE LOST ALL MY
THINGS, ONE IN EVERY PLACE
I'VE VISITED. NOW YOU HAVE
TO GO BACK AND FIND
THEM. AND SOMEWHERE ONE
OF THE WALDO-WATCHERS
HAS LOST THE POM-POM
FROM HIS HAT. CAN YOU
SPOT WHICH ONE, AND FIND
THE MISSING POM-POM?

Waldo

TO:
WALDO-FUN LOVERS
BACK TO THE BEGINNING,
START AGAIN,
TERRIFIC

WHERE
FAIRGROUND
WALDO?

2,000 YEARS AGO

FVN AND GAMES IN ANCIENT ROME

THE ROMANS SPENT MOST OF THEIR TIME FIGHTING, CONQVERING, LEARNING LATIN, AND MAKING ROADS. WHEN THEY TOOK THEIR HOLIDAYS THEY ALSO HAD GAMES AT THE COLISEVM (AN OLD SORT OF PLAYGROVND). THEIR FAVORITE GAMES WERE FIGHTING, MORE FIGHTING, CHARIOT RACING, FIGHTING, AND FEEDING CHRISTIANS TO LIONS. WHEN THE CROWD GAVE A GLADIATOR THE THVMBS-DOWN, IT MEANT HE SHOULD KILL HIS OPPONENT. A THVMBS-UP MEANT HE SHOULD LET HIM GO—TO FIGHT TO THE DEATH ANOTHER DAY.

1,003 YEARS AGO

ON TOUR WITH THE VIKINGS

At home, the Vikings were quiet people who liked knitting, cheese tasting, and boring things like that. But on tour, they went wild. They put on their best horned hats and sailed across the sea, singing and shouting like mad. If you heard them coming, it was best to run away, because once they had arrived and unpacked their axes, there was no holding them back.

800 YEARS AGO

Chaos at the Castle

Castles were built all across Europe, and the people living in them often had a beautiful view of the countryside. Unfortunately, they might also have had a view of an army laying siege to their castle. Luckily, when these besieging armies finally ran out of clean tights and tunics, they returned home. For years afterward, the knights told stories of the spectacular castles they had battered and bashed and the fascinating people they had captured — and wondered why they were never invited to parties!

600 YEARS AGO

ONCE UPON A SATURDAY MORNING

The Middle Ages were a very merry time to be alive, especially on Saturdays. Short skirts and striped tights were in fashion for men, everybody knew lots of jokes, and there was widespread juggling, jousting, archery, jesting, and fun. But if you got into trouble, the Middle Ages could be miserable. For the man in the stocks or the pillory or about to lose his head, Saturday morning was no laughing matter.

THE LAST DAYS OF THE AZTECS

The Aztecs lived in sunny Mexico and were rich and strong and liked swinging from poles, pretending to be eagles. They also liked making human sacrifices to their gods, so it was best to agree with everything they said. The Spanish were also rich and strong, and some of them, called conquistadors, came to Mexico in 1519 to have an adventure.

However, when the Aztecs and Spanish met, they did not agree on much.

400 YEARS AGO

Is red better than blue? What do you mean, your poem about cherry blossoms is better than mine? Shall we have another cup of tea? Over difficult questions such as these, the Japanese fought fiercely for hundreds of years. The fiercest fighters of all were the samurai, who wore flags on their backs so that their mommies could find them. The fighters without flags were called ashigaru. They couldn't take a joke any better than the samurai, especially about not having flags.

TROUBLE IN OLD JAPAN

250 YEARS AGO

BEING A PIRATE
(Shiver-me-timbers!)

It was really a lot of fun being a pirate, especially if you were very hairy and didn't have much in the way of brains. It also helped if you had a peg leg, an eye patch, a bandana, a pirate's hat with your name tag sewn inside, a treasure map, and a rusty cutlass. Once there were lots of pirates, but they died out in the end because too many of them were men (which is not a good idea).

HAVING A BALL IN GAYE PAREE

The history of France has some very bad parts, like getting your head chopped off by Madame Guillotine in the French Revolution, and some very good parts, like the invention of smelly cheese. In 1870, Napoleon (the third one) threw a marvelous ball in Paris to celebrate—1870 being a good part. All the beautiful people came and danced the night away to a band called the Third Republic.

THE GOLD RUSH

were frequently to be seen **RUSHING** toward **HOLES** in the ground, hoping to find **GOLD**. Most of them never even found the holes in the ground. But at least they all got some **EXERCISE** and **FRESH AIR** which kept them **HEALTHY**. And health is much more important than **GOLD** . . . isn't it?

At the end of the nineteenth century, large numbers of excited **AMERICANS**

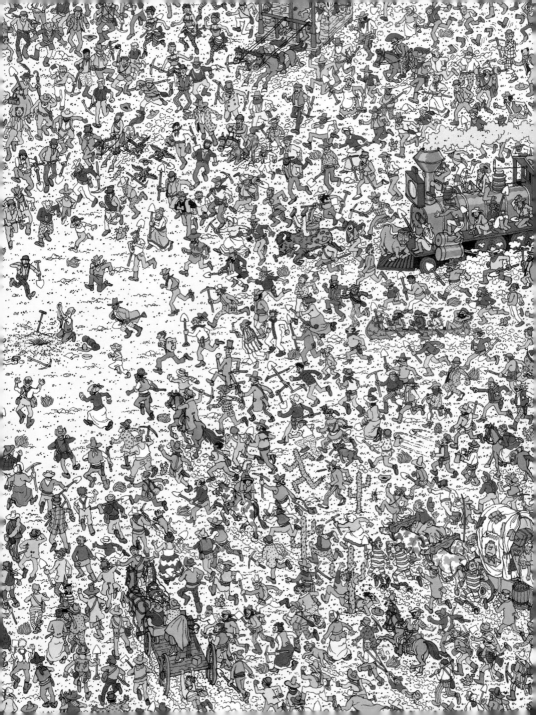

WALDO IS LOST
IN THE FUTURE!
FIND HIM! RESCUE HIM!
WALDO'S BOOKS ARE LOST
IN THE PAST!
FIND THEM! RESCUE THEM!
THERE'S ONE LOST IN EACH
PICTURE. GO BACK
AND LOOK FOR THEM!
WHERE'S WALDO?
WHERE'S WALDO
NOW?

THE GOBBLING GLUTTONS

ONCE UPON A TIME, WALDO
EMBARKED UPON A FANTASTIC
JOURNEY. FIRST, AMONG A
THRONG OF GOBBLING GLUTTONS,
HE MET WIZARD WHITEBEARD, WHO
COMMANDED HIM TO FIND A SCROLL AND
THEN TO FIND ANOTHER AT EVERY STAGE OF
HIS JOURNEY, FOR WHEN HE HAD FOUND
12 SCROLLS, HE WOULD UNDERSTAND THE
TRUTH ABOUT HIMSELF.

IN EVERY PICTURE, FIND WALDO, WOOF (BUT ALL
YOU CAN SEE IS HIS TAIL), WENDA, WIZARD
WHITEBEARD, ODLAW, AND THE SCROLL. THEN
FIND WALDO'S KEY, WOOF'S BONE (IN THIS SCENE
IT'S THE BONE THAT'S NEAREST TO HIS TAIL),
WENDA'S CAMERA, AND ODLAW'S BINOCULARS.

THERE ARE ALSO 25 WALDO-WATCHERS, EACH OF
WHOM APPEARS ONLY ONCE SOMEWHERE IN
THE FOLLOWING 12 PICTURES. AND ONE MORE
THING! CAN YOU FIND ANOTHER CHARACTER,
NOT SHOWN BELOW, WHO APPEARS ONCE IN
EVERY PICTURE EXCEPT THE LAST?

THE BATTLING MONKS

THEN WALDO AND WIZARD WHITEBEARD CAME
TO THE PLACE WHERE THE INVISIBLE MONKS
OF FIRE FOUGHT THE MONKS OF WATER. AND
AS WALDO SEARCHED FOR THE SECOND SCROLL,
HE SAW THAT MANY WALDOS HAD BEEN THIS WAY BEFORE.
AND WHEN HE FOUND THE SCROLL, IT WAS TIME TO
CONTINUE WITH HIS JOURNEY.

THE DRAGON FLYERS

THEN WALDO AND WHITEBEARD CAME TO THE LAND OF THE DRAGON FLYERS, WHERE MANY WALDOS HAD BEEN BEFORE. AND WALDO SAW A COLORFUL FLOCK OF DRAGONS, WITH FLYERS WEARING DRAGON-TAIL HOODS, FILLING THE SKY. THERE ARE ARROW SHAPES APLENTY TO SPOT IN THIS TALE OF TAILS, O BRAINY DRAGON WATCHERS. AND WHEN WALDO FOUND THE THIRD SCROLL, IT WAS TIME TO CONTINUE HIS JOURNEY.

THE GREAT BALLGAME PLAYERS

THEN WALDO AND WIZARD WHITEBEARD CAME TO THE PLAYING FIELD OF THE GREAT BALLGAME PLAYERS, WHERE MANY WALDOS HAD BEEN BEFORE. AND WALDO SAW THAT FOUR TEAMS WERE PLAYING AGAINST ONE ANOTHER (BUT WAS ANYONE WINNING? WHAT WAS THE SCORE? CAN YOU WORK OUT THE RULES?). THEN WALDO FOUND THE FOURTH SCROLL AND CONTINUED WITH HIS JOURNEY.

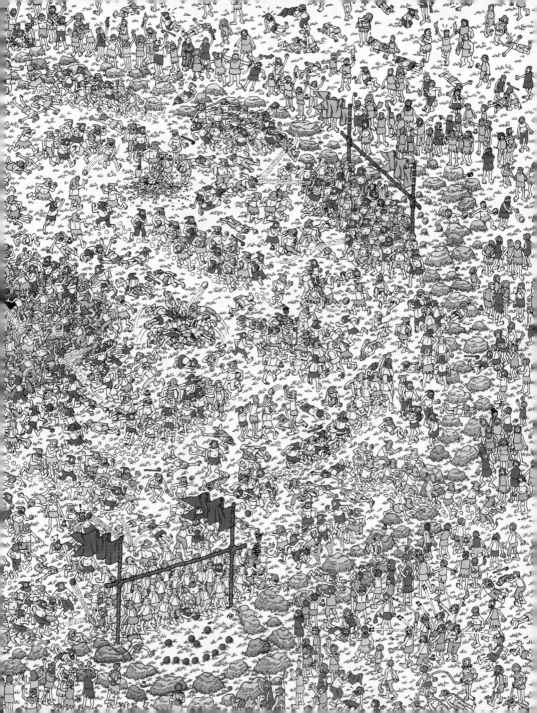

THE FEROCIOUS RED DWARFS

THEN WALDO AND WIZARD WHITEBEARD CAME AMONG THE FEROCIOUS RED DWARFS, WHERE MANY WALDOS HAD BEEN BEFORE. AND THE DWARFS WERE ATTACKING THE MANY-COLORED SPEARMEN, CAUSING MIGHTY MAYHEM AND HORRID HAVOC. AND WALDO FOUND THE FIFTH SCROLL AND CONTINUED WITH HIS JOURNEY.

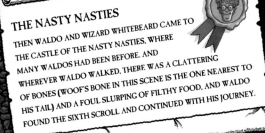

THE NASTY NASTIES

THEN WALDO AND WIZARD WHITEBEARD CAME TO
THE CASTLE OF THE NASTY NASTIES, WHERE
MANY WALDOS HAD BEEN BEFORE. AND
WHEREVER WALDO WALKED, THERE WAS A CLATTERING
OF BONES (WOOF'S BONE IN THIS SCENE IS THE ONE NEAREST TO
HIS TAIL) AND A FOUL SLURPING OF FILTHY FOOD, AND WALDO
FOUND THE SIXTH SCROLL AND CONTINUED WITH HIS JOURNEY.

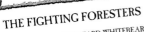

THE FIGHTING FORESTERS

THEN WALDO AND WIZARD WHITEBEARD CAME
AMONG THE FIGHTING FORESTERS, WHERE
MANY WALDOS HAD BEEN BEFORE. AND IN THEIR
BATTLE WITH THE EVIL BLACK KNIGHTS, THE
FOREST WOMEN WERE AIDED BY THE ANIMALS, BY THE LIVING
MUD, EVEN BY THE TREES THEMSELVES. AND WALDO FOUND
THE SEVENTH SCROLL AND CONTINUED WITH HIS JOURNEY.

THE DEEP-SEA DIVERS

THEN WALDO AND WIZARD WHITEBEARD CAME TO THE WATERY WORLD OF THE DEEP-SEA DIVERS, WHERE MANY WALDOS HAD BEEN BEFORE. AND WALDO SEARCHED FOR THE EIGHTH SCROLL AMONG THE MONSTERS OF THE DEEP, AMONG THE MERMAIDS, FISHERMEN, AND FISH. AND WHEN HE FOUND IT, IT WAS TIME TO CONTINUE WITH HIS JOURNEY.

THE KNIGHTS OF THE MAGIC FLAG

THEN WALDO AND WIZARD WHITEBEARD CAME
TO A PLACE MORE CROWDED THAN ANY WALDO
HAD SEEN BEFORE, WHERE TWO ARMIES WITH
MANY MAGIC FLAGS WERE LOCKED IN COMBAT.
AND WALDO SAW THAT MANY WALDOS HAD BEEN THIS WAY
BEFORE. AND WHEN HE FOUND THE NINTH SCROLL, IT WAS
TIME TO CONTINUE WITH HIS JOURNEY.

THE UNFRIENDLY GIANTS

THEN WALDO AND WIZARD WHITEBEARD CAME TO
THE LAND OF THE UNFRIENDLY GIANTS, WHERE
MANY WALDOS HAD BEEN BEFORE. AND WALDO
SAW THAT THE GIANTS WERE HORRIDLY
HARASSING THE LITTLE PEOPLE. AND WHEN HE FOUND THE
TENTH SCROLL, IT WAS TIME TO CONTINUE WITH HIS JOURNEY.

THE UNDERGROUND HUNTERS

THEN WALDO AND WIZARD WHITEBEARD CAME
AMONG THE UNDERGROUND HUNTERS, WHERE
MANY WALDOS HAD BEEN BEFORE. THERE
WAS MUCH MENACE IN THIS PLACE, AND A
MULTITUDE OF MALEVOLENT MONSTERS. WALDO
FOUND THE ELEVENTH SCROLL AND CONTINUED
WITH HIS JOURNEY.

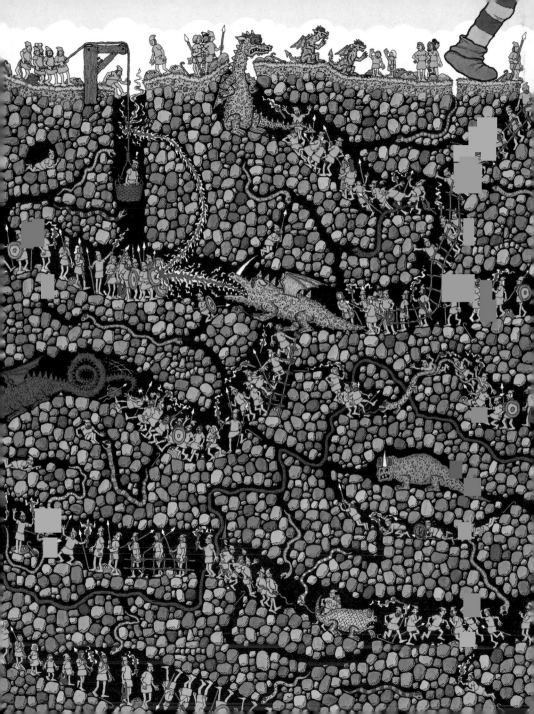

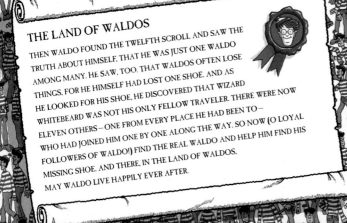

THE LAND OF WALDOS

THEN WALDO FOUND THE TWELFTH SCROLL AND SAW THE TRUTH ABOUT HIMSELF, THAT HE WAS JUST ONE WALDO AMONG MANY. HE SAW, TOO, THAT WALDOS OFTEN LOSE THINGS, FOR HE HIMSELF HAD LOST ONE SHOE. AND AS HE LOOKED FOR HIS SHOE, HE DISCOVERED THAT WIZARD WHITEBEARD WAS NOT HIS ONLY FELLOW TRAVELER. THERE WERE NOW ELEVEN OTHERS — ONE FROM EVERY PLACE HE HAD BEEN TO — WHO HAD JOINED HIM ONE BY ONE ALONG THE WAY. SO NOW (O LOYAL FOLLOWERS OF WALDO!) FIND THE REAL WALDO AND HELP HIM FIND HIS MISSING SHOE. AND THERE, IN THE LAND OF WALDOS, MAY WALDO LIVE HAPPILY EVER AFTER.

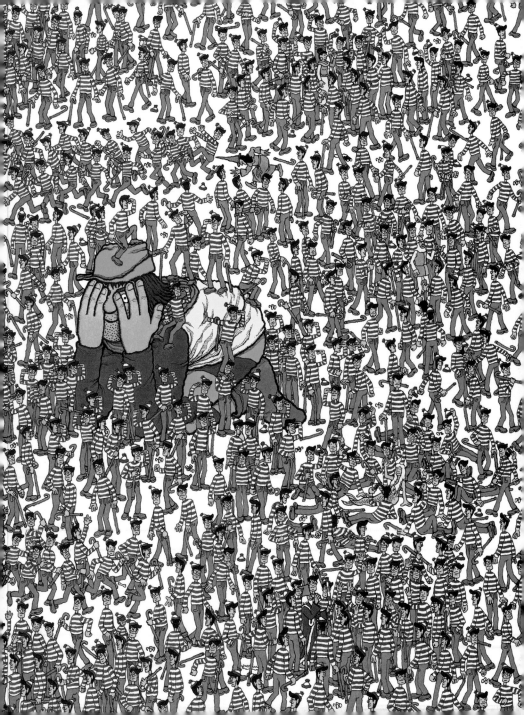

A DREAM COME TRUE

WOW, WALDO-WATCHERS, THIS IS FANTASTIC. I'M REALLY IN HOLLYWOOD! LOOK AT THE FILM PEOPLE EVERYWHERE—I WONDER WHAT MOVIES THEY'RE MAKING. THIS IS MY DREAM COME TRUE . . . TO MEET THE DIRECTORS AND ACTORS, TO WALK THROUGH THE CROWDS OF EXTRAS, TO SEE BEHIND THE SCENES! PHEW, I WONDER IF I'LL APPEAR IN A MOVIE MYSELF!

★ ★ ★ ★ WHAT TO LOOK FOR IN HOLLYWOOD! ★ ★ ★ ★

WELCOME TO TINSELTOWN, WALDO-WATCHERS! THESE ARE THE PEOPLE AND THINGS TO LOOK FOR AS YOU WALK THROUGH THE FILM SETS WITH WALDO.

★ FIRST (OF COURSE!) WHERE'S WALDO?

★ NEXT FIND WALDO'S CANINE COMPANION, WOOF—REMEMBER, ALL YOU CAN SEE IS HIS TAIL!

★ THEN FIND WALDO'S FRIEND WENDA!

★ ABRACADABRA! NOW FOCUS IN ON WIZARD WHITEBEARD!

★ BOO! HISS! HERE COMES THE BAD GUY, ODLAW!

★ NOW SPOT THESE 25 WALDO-WATCHERS, EACH OF WHOM APPEARS ONLY ONCE BEFORE THE FINAL FANTASTIC SCENE!

★ WOW! INCREDIBLE! SPOT ONE OTHER CHARACTER WHO APPEARS IN EVERY SCENE EXCEPT THE LAST!

★ ★ KEEP ON SEARCHING! THERE'S MORE TO FIND! ★ ★

ON EVERY SET, FIND WALDO'S LOST KEY!
WOOF'S LOST BONE! WENDA'S LOST CAMERA! WIZARD WHITEBEARD'S SCROLL!
ODLAW'S LOST BINOCULARS! AND A MISSING CAN OF FILM!

★ ★ ★ ★ ★ ★ AND MORE AND MORE! ★ ★ ★ ★ ★ ★

EACH OF THE FOUR POSTERS ON THE WALL OVER THERE IS PART OF ONE OF THE FILM SETS WALDO IS ABOUT TO VISIT. ★ FIND OUT WHERE THE POSTERS CAME FROM. ★ THEN SPOT ANY DIFFERENCES BETWEEN THE POSTERS AND THE SETS.

SHHH! THIS IS A SILENT MOVIE

SO THIS IS HOW THE HOLLYWOOD DREAM BEGAN-WITH SILENT MOVIES MADE IN BLACK AND WHITE. IT LOOKS CRAZY AND IT MAKES YOU LAUGH. ACTING IN SLAPSTICK COMEDIES MUST BE REALLY HARD-LOOK HOW MANY ACCIDENTS ARE HAPPENING. BUT THE GREAT THING IS THAT NONE OF THE ACTORS EVER GET HURT, HOWEVER OFTEN THEY FALL FLAT ON THEIR FACES!

FUN IN THE FOREIGN LEGION

PHEW, MOVIE FANS, DON'T GET OVERHEATED, THIS IS THE MOST SIZZLING LOCATION SO FAR! EVERYONE'S SWELTERING, FROM STARS TO SAND-SHIFTERS. SOME OF THOSE EXTRAS LOOK LIKE THEY'RE LOSING THEIR COOL—HAVE THEY FORGOTTEN THIS IS ONLY A MOVIE? PERHAPS IT'S TIME A FEW MORE OF THEM DESERTED THE DESERT AND JOINED THE RUSH FOR ICE CREAM!

CAVE OF THE PLUNDERING PIRATES

WHAT A PLETHORA OF PLUNDERING PIRATES, WALDO-WATCHERS! WHAT A CRUSH IN THE CAVE! THERE MUST BE TONS OF TREATS AND TRINKETS IN THIS TEEMING TREASURE TROVE, WITH SPOOKY SPIRITS CENTER STAGE AND PIRATICAL PILFERERS TO SPOT, THE DIRECTOR CERTAINLY HAS HIS HANDS FULL. LET'S HOPE HE HAS THE GOLDEN TOUCH! SHIVER-ME-TIMBERS, WHAT A FEARFULLY FUNNY FLICK THIS IS!

THE SWASHBUCKLING MUSKETEERS

ALL FOR ONE, ONE FOR ALL! WASN'T THAT THE MOTTO OF THE THREE MUSKETEERS? NOW, LOOK AT THIS FREE-FOR-ALL! CAN YOU SPOT OUR THREE GALLANT HEROES BATTLING WITH THE RED-COATED CARDINAL'S GUARDS? WITH ALL THIS SWASHBUCKLING ACTION GOING ON, I WONDER HOW THE CAMERAMEN CAN CAPTURE IT ALL ON FILM!

DINOSAURS, SPACEMEN, AND GHOULS

PHEW, INCREDIBLE! TIME, SPACE, AND HORROR ARE IN A MIGHTY MUDDLE HERE! WHAT COSMIC COSTUMES AND WHAT GREAT SPECIAL EFFECTS! ONE OF THOSE FLYING SAUCERS LOOKS LIKE IT'S REALLY FLYING! ARE THOSE REAL ALIENS INSIDE, NOT ACTORS AT ALL? SO WHAT'S REAL AND WHAT'S MADE UP IN FILMS LIKE THESE?

ROBIN HOOD'S MERRY MESS-UP

LOOK HOW MANY MERRY MEN HAVE LEFT SHERWOOD FOREST FOR A DAY OUT IN NOTTINGHAM CASTLE! AND WHAT A MERRY TIME THEY'RE HAVING, MESSING UP THE SHERIFF'S PARADE. WHICH ONE IS ROBIN HOOD? THE ONE WEARING A ROBIN HOOD, OF COURSE! WHEN YOU GO TO SEE THIS MOVIE, YOU'LL THINK IT'S ALL REAL, BUT THE CASTLE'S STONE WALLS ARE MADE OF WOOD!

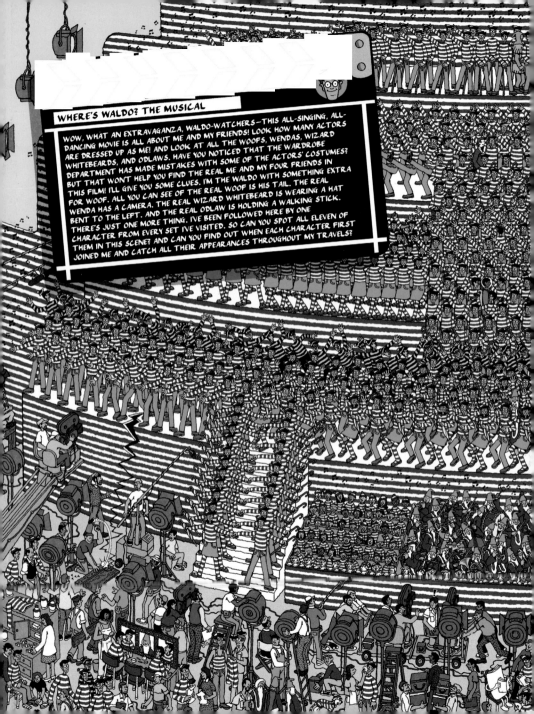

WHERE'S WALDO? THE MUSICAL

WOW, WHAT AN EXTRAVAGANZA, WALDO-WATCHERS—THIS ALL-SINGING, ALL-DANCING MOVIE IS ALL ABOUT ME AND MY FRIENDS! LOOK HOW MANY ACTORS ARE DRESSED UP AS ME! AND LOOK AT ALL THE WOOFS, WENDAS, WIZARD WHITEBEARDS, AND ODLAWS. HAVE YOU NOTICED THAT THE WARDROBE DEPARTMENT HAS MADE MISTAKES WITH SOME OF THE ACTORS' COSTUMES? BUT THAT WON'T HELP YOU FIND THE REAL ME AND MY FOUR FRIENDS IN THIS FILM! I'LL GIVE YOU SOME CLUES. I'M THE WALDO WITH SOMETHING EXTRA FOR WOOF. ALL YOU CAN SEE OF THE REAL WOOF IS HIS TAIL. THE REAL WENDA HAS A CAMERA. THE REAL WIZARD WHITEBEARD IS WEARING A HAT BENT TO THE LEFT. AND THE REAL ODLAW IS HOLDING A WALKING STICK. THERE'S JUST ONE MORE THING. I'VE BEEN FOLLOWED HERE BY ONE CHARACTER FROM EVERY SET I'VE VISITED. SO CAN YOU SPOT ALL ELEVEN OF THEM IN THIS SCENE? AND CAN YOU FIND OUT WHEN EACH CHARACTER FIRST JOINED ME AND CATCH ALL THEIR APPEARANCES THROUGHOUT MY TRAVELS?

ONCE UPON A PAGE...

HEY, WALDO FANS! LOOK AT ALL THESE BRILLIANT BOOKS! LOOK AT ALL THE CHARACTERS WHO HAVE STEPPED OUT FROM THEIR PAGES! WOW! WHAT A MAGIC SCENE! THESE BOOKS HAVE REALLY COME ALIVE! FANTASTIC — THAT BOOK OVER THERE IS ABOUT MY TRAVELS! AND WOOF, WENDA, WIZARD WHITEBEARD, AND ODLAW ALL HAVE SPECIAL BOOKS OF THEIR OWN. NOW YOU CAN JOIN US TOO, IF YOU CAN FIND US, AND WE'LL TRAVEL TOGETHER THROUGH ALL THE OTHER WONDERFUL SCENES IN THIS WONDER BOOK. ONE SCENE IS MY SPECIAL FAVORITE — YOU'LL NEVER GUESS WHAT MAKES IT SO GREAT. THE BOOKMARK MARKS IT, SO WHEN WE GET THERE, YOU WILL KNOW. NOW GET SEARCHING, WALDO-FOLLOWERS, AND OFF WE GO! AND BE PREPARED FOR LOTS OF SURPRISES ALONG THE WAY!

Waldo

THE SEARCH IS ON! FIND THESE FIVE INTREPID TRAVELERS IN EVERY SCENE IN THE WONDER BOOK!

- FIND WALDO . . . WHO LEADS THE WAY!
- FIND WOOF . . . WHO WAGS HIS TAIL!
  (WHICH IS USUALLY ALL YOU CAN SEE!)
- FIND WENDA . . . WHO TAKES THE PICTURES!
- FIND WIZARD WHITEBEARD . . . WHO CASTS THE SPELLS!
- FIND ODLAW . . . WHOSE GOOD DEEDS ARE FEW INDEED!

THE SEARCH CONTINUES! NEXT FIND THESE IMPORTANT THINGS THE TRAVELERS HAVE LOST!

- FIND WALDO'S LOST KEY!
- FIND WOOF'S LOST BONE!
- FIND WENDA'S LOST CAMERA!
- FIND WIZARD WHITEBEARD'S MAGIC SCROLL!
- FIND ODLAW'S LOST BINOCULARS!

THE GREAT BOOK OF ODLAW'S GOOD DEEDS

CLASSIC STORIES FROM LITERATURE

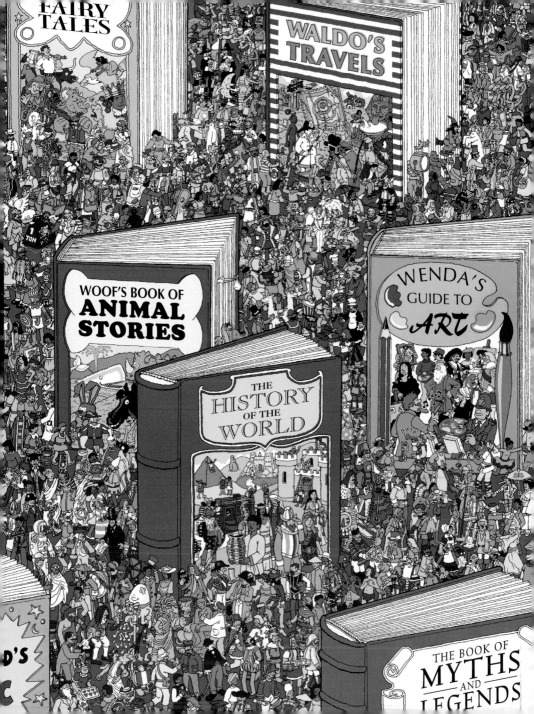

THE MIGHTY FRUIT FIGHT

WOW! AMAZING! HAVE YOU EVER IN YOUR LIVES SEEN A PLACE SO FULL OF FRUIT? HOW SWEET IT IS TO SAIL LEMON BOATS DOWN ORANGE JUICE RIVERS! BUT WATCH OUT, WALDO FANS! THE APPLES HAVE TURNED SOUR AND THEY'RE ATTACKING ALL THE OTHER FRUIT. WHOOSH! SQUIRT! SPLOOOOOSH! THERE'S A FRUIT JAM IN THE RIVER, SCUFFLES ON THE BANANA BRIDGES, AND SUGAR BEING POURED ALL OVER THE STRAWBERRIES! PHEW! WHAT A MIGHTY FRUIT FIGHT!

THE GAME OF GAMES

Four huge teams are playing this great game of games. The referees are trying to see that no one breaks the rules. Between the starting line at the top and the finish line at the bottom, there are lots of puzzles, booby traps, and tests. The green team's nearly won, and the orange team's hardly started! Can you spot the only orange team player who has finished? And the only green team player who has not yet begun?

TOYS! TOYS! TOYS!

WOW! ALL THE TEENY-TINY TOY CREATURES ARE COMING OUT OF THE TOY BOX TO EXPLORE THE PLAYROOM! THE BOOKS ARE TOO HUGE TO READ, BUT THE GREEN ONE IS PERFECT AS A SOCCER FIELD! SWOOSH! AND THE BOOKMARK MAKES A GREAT SLIDE! CAN YOU SEE A TEDDY TAKING OFF IN A PAPER PLANE? AND A DINOSAUR CHASING A CAVEMAN?

WHAT HIGH JINKS AND HIGH-WIRE ACTS ARE HAPPENING HERE! SO DO YOU THINK THAT THE TOYS ALWAYS HAVE GREAT TIMES LIKE THESE WHEN NO ONE IS AROUND?

BRIGHT LIGHTS
AND
NIGHT FRIGHTS

Hey! What blazing beams of light, what a dazzling display! Glitter, twinkle, sparkle, flash—look how brightly these lighthouses light up the night! But, oh no, the monsters want to put the lights out! They're attacking from all sides. The sailors are squirting pink goo at them, but

the monsters spurt green goo right back! But wait! Three of the monsters are firing different colored goo! Splash, splat, splurge! Can you see them, Waldo-watchers?

THE CAKE FACTORY

MMMM! FEAST YOUR EYES, WALDO-WATCHERS! SNIFF THE DELICIOUS SMELLS OF BAKING CAKES! DROOL AT THE TASTY TOPPINGS! CAN YOU SEE A CAKE LIKE A TEAPOT, A CAKE LIKE A HOUSE, A CAKE SO TALL A WORKER ON THE FLOOR ABOVE IS LICKING IT? CAKES, CAKES, EVERYWHERE! HOW SCRUMPTIOUS! HOW YUM-YUM-YUMPTIOUS! LOOK AT THE OOZING SUGAR ICING AND THE SHINY RED CHERRIES ON THE ROOF UP THERE! THAT ROOM IS WHERE THE FACTORY CONTROLLERS WORK, BUT HAVE THEY LOST CONTROL?

THE ODLAW SWAMP

THE BRAVE ARMY OF MANY HATS IS TRYING TO GET THROUGH THIS FEARFUL SWAMP. HUNDREDS OF ODLAWS AND BLACK-AND-YELLOW SWAMP CREATURES ARE CAUSING TROUBLE IN THE UNDERGROWTH. THE REAL ODLAW IS THE ONE CLOSEST TO HIS LOST PAIR OF BINOCULARS. CAN YOU FIND HIM, X-RAY-EYED ONES? HOW MANY DIFFERENT KINDS OF HATS CAN YOU SEE ON THE SOLDIERS' HEADS? SQUELCH! SQUELCH! I'M GLAD I'M NOT IN THEIR SHOES! ESPECIALLY AS THEIR FEET ARE IN THE MURKY MUD!

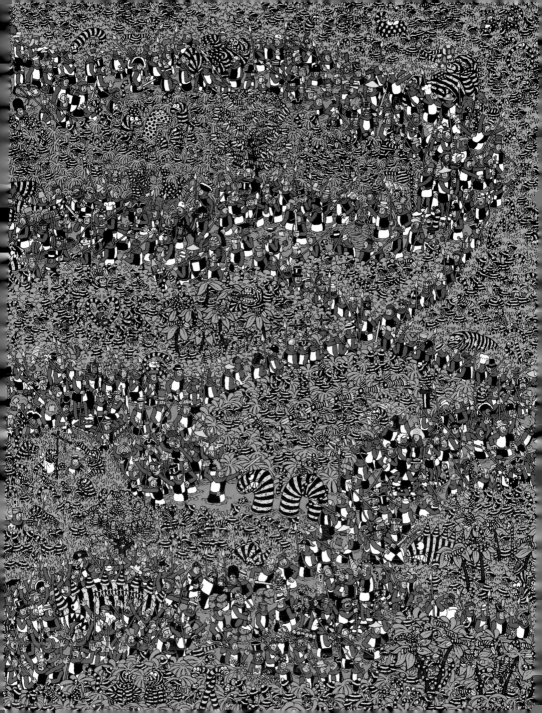

THE FANTASTIC FLOWER GARDEN

WOW! WHAT A BRIGHT AND DAZZLING GARDEN SPECTACLE! ALL THE FLOWERS ARE IN FULL BLOOM, AND HUNDREDS OF BUSY GARDENERS ARE WATERING AND TENDING THEM. THE PETAL COSTUMES THEY ARE WEARING MAKE THEM LOOK LIKE FLOWERS THEMSELVES! VEGETABLES ARE GROWING IN THE GARDEN TOO. HOW MANY DIFFERENT KINDS

CAN YOU SEE? SNIFF THE AIR, WALDO-FOLLOWERS! SMELL THE FANTASTIC SCENTS! WHAT A TREAT FOR YOUR NOSES AS WELL AS YOUR EYES!

THE CORRIDORS OF TIME

TICK-TOCK, TICK-TOCK! THE HANDS OF ALL THE CLOCKS EXCEPT ONE SAY A QUARTER TO TWELVE. WHAT A DING-DONG THERE WILL BE WHEN THEY STRIKE! CAN YOU FIND THE ONLY CLOCK THAT TELLS A DIFFERENT TIME? IN THIS SCENE ARE THIRTY-NINE DOORS. ABOVE EACH DOOR APPEARS THE SHAPE OF THE KEY THAT WILL UNLOCK IT. CAN YOU FIND THE KEYS IN THE CROWD, BRAINY ONES, AND MATCH THEM TO THE SHAPES? OH, NO! ONE DOOR HAS NO SHAPE ABOVE IT! EVEN SO, YOU MUST FIND ITS KEY!

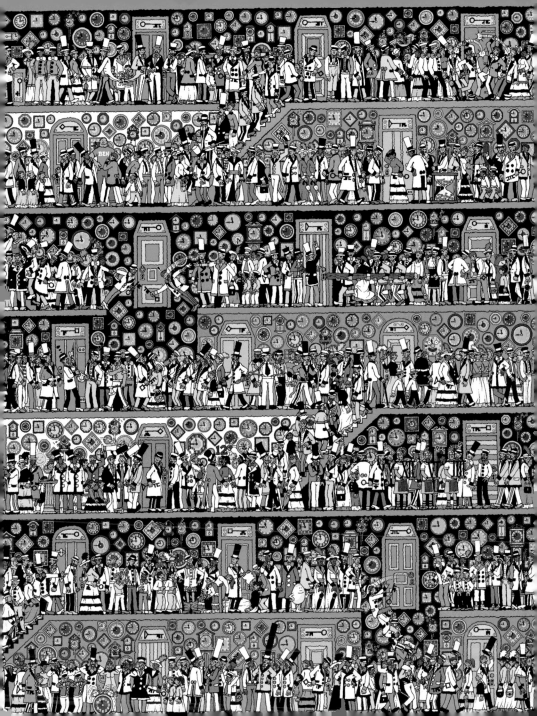

THE LAND
OF
WOOFS

HEY! LOOK AT ALL THESE DOGS THAT ARE DRESSED LIKE WOOF! BOW WOW WOW! IN THIS LAND, A DOG'S LIFE IS THE HIGHLIFE! THERE'S A LUXURY WOOF HOTEL WITH A BONE-SHAPED SWIMMING POOL, AND AT THE WOOF RACETRACK, LOTS OF WOOFS ARE CHASING ATTENDANTS DRESSED AS CATS, SAUSAGES, AND POSTMEN! THE BOOKMARK IS ON THIS PAGE, WALDO-FOLLOWERS. SO NOW YOU KNOW, THIS IS MY FAVORITE SCENE! THIS IS THE ONLY SCENE IN THE BOOK WHERE YOU CAN SEE MORE OF THE REAL WOOF THAN JUST HIS TAIL! BUT CAN YOU FIND HIM? HE'S THE ONLY ONE WITH FIVE RED STRIPES ON HIS TAIL! HERE'S ANOTHER CHALLENGE! ELEVEN TRAVELERS

HAVE FOLLOWED ME HERE — ONE FROM EVERY SCENE. CAN YOU SEE THEM? AND CAN YOU FIND WHERE EACH ONE JOINED ME ON MY ADVENTURES, AND SPOT ALL THEIR APPEARANCES AFTERWARD? KEEP ON SEARCHING, WALDO FANS! HAVE A WONDERFUL, WONDERFUL TIME!

THE GREAT PICTURE HUNT!

HEY, WALDO FANS, WELCOME TO THE GREAT PICTURE HUNT!

THE FUN STARTS IN EXHIBIT 1, ODLAW'S PICTURE PANDEMONIUM, WHERE YOU'LL FIND 30 ENORMOUS PORTRAITS. WOW! EXAMINE THEM CAREFULLY, BECAUSE EVERY ONE OF THE PORTRAIT SUBJECTS CAN BE FOUND SOMEWHERE ELSE IN THIS BOOK ... BUT ONLY ONCE. YOUR CHALLENGE IS TO FIND THESE SLIPPERY SUBJECTS WHEREVER THEY MIGHT BE HIDING.

ARE YOU READY FOR AN ART ADVENTURE GALLERY GAZERS? HAVE FUN!

Waldo

EXHIBIT 1—ODLAW'S PICTURE PANDEMONIUM

WOW, WALDO FANS, WHAT PORTRAIT PANDEMONIUM! HAVE YOU EVER SEEN SO MANY YELLOW AND BLACK STRIPES IN ONE PLACE? STRIPE-TASTIC! WE'RE HERE IN ODLAW'S PICTURE GALLERY, AND JUST LOOK AT WHAT HIS ARTFUL ASSOCIATES HAVE CARRIED IN—30 PECULIAR PORTRAITS IN AN ODDITY OF FRAMES. AMAZING! THERE'S QUITE A CAST OF CHARACTERS IN THESE PAINTINGS, AND THEY ALL APPEAR AGAIN ELSEWHERE IN THE BOOK. AND PICTURE THIS: ONE OF THEM EVEN APPEARS SOMEWHERE IN THIS CRAZY CROWD! GOOD LUCK ON YOUR HUNT FOR THE PLACES WITH THE FACES. WHAT A PICTURE!

EXHIBIT 2 —
A SPORTING LIFE
WELCOME, PICTURE HUNT PALS, TO MY
SPECIAL REPORT FROM THE LAND OF
SPORTS. FANTASTIC! IT'S LIKE THE OLYMPICS
EVERY DAY HERE, BUT WITH SO MANY
ATHLETIC EVENTS ON THE MENU, THERE'S NO
TIME LEFT FOR ANY REST AND RELAXATION.
BUT THERE'S NOTHING TOO STRENUOUS
ABOUT OUR MAIN EVENT, THE GREAT
PICTURE HUNT, SO KEEP YOUR EYES ON
THE BALL AND YOUR POINTER
FINGER READY. ON YOUR
MARK, GET SET, GO!

EXHIBIT 5—THE PINK PARADISE PARTY

IT'S SATURDAY NIGHT, THE TEMPERATURE IS RISING, AND IT LOOKS AS IF A RASH OF MUSICAL MAYHEM AND DISCO FEVER HAS BROKEN OUT IN THIS DIZZY DANCE HALL. WHEW! IT'S HOT! HIP HIP-HOPPERS, ROCK-AND-ROLLERS, AND BODY-AND-SOULERS—IT'S A PACKED-OUT, PARTYGOERS' PINK PARADISE. SO GET ON DOWN, CUT YOUR GROOVE, AND MAKE YOUR MOVES—IT'S TIME TO SHUFFLE YOUR FEET TO THE PICTURE HUNT BEAT!

EXHIBIT 6 — OLD FRIENDS

AH, PICTURE HUNT PALS, HOW I LOVE TO LOOK THROUGH MY SCRAPBOOKS OF MEMORIES AND SOUVENIRS. THIS PAGE IS ONE OF MY FAVORITES: A COLLAGE CRAMMED WITH FAMILIAR FACES FROM MY EARLIER ADVENTURES. FANTASTIC! EVEN THE MOST DEDICATED OF WALDO-WATCHERS AMONG YOU MAY HAVE TROUBLE RECOGNIZING ALL THE OLD FRIENDS HERE— IT'S QUITE A CHALLENGE. BUT HERE'S AN EASIER TEASER THAT ANYONE CAN DO: JUST LOOK AT THE CIRCLED FACES IN THE BORDER OF THIS FRAME, THEN SEE IF YOU CAN SPOT THEM IN THE SURROUNDING PICTURE.

EXHIBIT 8—THE MONSTER MASTERPIECE

YIKES, SPIKES, AND SCALY SEGMENTS, I'M LOST IN THE LAND OF THE MONSTERS. WHAT A CREATURE FEATURE! WHO'S IN CHARGE HERE, ANYWAY? THE HELMETED HUNTERS OR THEIR QUARRELSOME QUARRY? YOU'D BETTER WATCH OUT FOR BOTH AS YOU DIVE INTO THIS MONSTER MAYHEM, ART FANS— THERE ARE STILL SOME PORTRAIT SUBJECTS TO FIND. WHAT A MONSTROSITY!

EXHIBIT 9—WALDOWORLD

WHAT A WEIRD AND WACKY WORLD WE'RE IN,
GALLERY GAZERS—NOT JUST A WORLD OF WALDOS
BUT A WORLD OF WHITEBEARDS, WENDAS, WOOFS, AND
AN ODDITY OF ODLAWS AS WELL. AMAZING! BUT LOOK
AGAIN. . . . THERE'S ONLY ONE REAL WALDO HERE, AND
THE SAME GOES FOR MY FRIENDS, TOO. DON'T FORGET
THAT YOU CAN TELL IF WE'RE THE GENUINE ARTICLES
BY OUR CORRECT ARRANGEMENT OF STRIPES. SO CAST
YOUR EYES ACROSS THIS COLLECTION OF IMPOSTERS AND
IMPERSONATORS AND SEE IF YOU CAN FIND THE REAL US!

EXHIBIT 10 — WALDOWORLD AGAIN

DON'T BE DAUNTED BY HAVING TO DALLY OVER THIS DIZZY DIORAMA OF DOPPELGANGERS, DEAR READERS. EVERYTHING IS NOT AS IT APPEARS. WE'RE ALL STILL HERE, BUT THIS TIME THERE ARE 20 VARIATIONS FROM THE SCENE ON THE LEFT. CAN YOU SPOT ALL THE DIFFERENCES? AND HAVE YOU FOUND THE REAL WHITEBEARD, WENDA, WOOF, AND ODLAW YET? IF YOU'RE STILL HAVING TROUBLE FINDING THE REAL US, WHY NOT CHECK OUT HOW WE LOOK IN THE KEY AT THE BEGINNING OF THE BOOK?

EXHIBIT 11—PIRATE PANORAMA

SHIVER ME TIMBERS, SHIPMATES, WHAT PERFIDIOUS PIRATE PANORAMA IS THIS? WOW! AMAZING! WE'VE SAILED THE SEVEN SEAS SEARCHING FOR THOSE 30 PESKY PORTRAIT PEOPLE, AND NOW THAT OUR JOURNEY IS ALMOST OVER, I JUST HOPE THE PIRATES DON'T MAKE THEM WALK THE PLANK! I'M SURE THEY WOULD RATHER BE MAROONED ON A DESERT ISLAND THAN MEET THESE BARMY BUCCANEERS. ALL HANDS ON DECK!

EXHIBIT 12—THE GREAT PORTRAIT EXHIBITION

OUR JOURNEY IS NOW OVER, WALDO FANS, BUT WHAT A FITTING FINALE—A FANTASTIC EXHIBITION IN A PROPER ART GALLERY! THE CROWD HERE SEEMS MORE WELCOMING THAN ODLAW'S ODD ENSEMBLE FROM THE FIRST SCENE. I'M ALSO REALLY PLEASED THAT ALL 30 OF THE CHARACTERS WE'VE BEEN SEARCHING FOR IN THE EARLIER SCENES APPEAR AGAIN HERE AMONG THE GALLERY GAZERS. SEE IF YOU CAN SPOT THEM AS THEY TRY TO BLEND INTO THE CROWD AND ENJOY THE SHOW. I HOPE YOU FOUND THEM IN THE PREVIOUS PAGES, TOO. IF NOT, THERE'S STILL PLENTY OF TIME TO DO SO—THE EXHIBITION NEVER CLOSES!

HI, WALDO-WATCHERS!

ARE YOU READY TO JOIN ME ON ANOTHER
INCREDIBLE ADVENTURE WITH MORE FUN
AND GAMES THAN EVER BEFORE?
I SEE SO MANY WONDERFUL THINGS ON MY
TRAVELS THAT THIS TIME I AM TAKING MY
NOTEPAD TO HELP ME REMEMBER THEM.
WOW! THE EXCITEMENT BEGINS RIGHT HERE,
AS THE RED KNIGHTS STORM THE BLUE KNIGHTS'
CASTLE WALLS. CAN YOU SPOT SOME GRINNING
GARGOYLES, A GHASTLY GHOST, AND A GIANT CAKE?
THE SEARCH IS ON!

Waldo

FIND WALDO, WOOF (BUT ALL YOU CAN SEE IS HIS TAIL), WENDA,
WIZARD WHITEBEARD AND ODLAW IN EVERY SCENE. (DON'T BE
FOOLED BY ANY CHILDREN THAT ARE DRESSED LIKE WALDO!)

FIND THE PRECIOUS THINGS THEY'VE LOST, TOO:
WALDO'S KEY, WOOF'S BONE, WENDA'S CAMERA, WIZARD
WHITEBEARD'S SCROLL, AND ODLAW'S BINOCULARS.

ONE MORE THING! CAN YOU FIND A PIECE OF PAPER THAT WALDO
HAS DROPPED FROM HIS NOTEPAD IN EVERY SCENE?

THE JURASSIC GAMES

GOODNESS CRETACEOUS! WHO WILL YOU SUPPORT FROM THE SIDELINES: THE BLUE STRIPY-SAURUS TEAM OR THE PINK SPOTTY-DOCUS TEAM? WILL YOU CHEER FOR CRICKET, ROWING, OR BASKETBALL? DON'T FORGET TO WAVE IF YOU SEE A T. REX — THEY'RE NOT ON ANY TEAM, BUT YOU WOULDN'T WANT TO GET ON THEIR BAD SIDE!

PICTURE THIS

PHEW! LOOK AT ALL THESE FRAMED PORTRAITS. ALTHOUGH THEY MAY BE COLORED DIFFERENTLY, SOME OF THESE ARE CHARACTERS I HAVE MET ON MY OTHER TRAVELS. THERE ARE ALSO SOME WHO APPEAR ELSEWHERE IN THIS BOOK. CAN YOU SPOT FOUR CHARACTERS THAT APPEAR TWICE IN THIS SPECTACULAR DISPLAY?

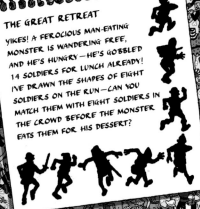

THE GREAT RETREAT

YIKES! A FEROCIOUS MAN-EATING MONSTER IS WANDERING FREE, AND HE'S HUNGRY—HE'S GOBBLED 14 SOLDIERS FOR LUNCH ALREADY! I'VE DRAWN THE SHAPES OF EIGHT SOLDIERS ON THE RUN—CAN YOU MATCH THEM WITH EIGHT SOLDIERS IN THE CROWD BEFORE THE MONSTER EATS THEM FOR HIS DESSERT?

WHAT A DOG FIGHT!

BOW WOW WOW! TWO ARMIES ARE LOCKED IN BATTLE, ALL WITH DOG MASKS ON. ONE ARMY IS DRESSED IN BLUE, BLACK, AND WHITE, AND THE OTHER IN RED, BROWN, AND CREAM. CAN YOU FIND EIGHT SOLDIERS, FOUR FROM EACH SIDE, WITH SOMETHING IN ONE OF THE OTHER SIDE'S COLORS? OH, AND WHERE IS WOOF IN THIS DOG PACK?

THE BEAT OF THE DRUMS

BOOM BOOM BADOOM! WHAT AN ORDERLY SCENE! TWO ARMIES ARE STANDING AT ATTENTION, SMARTLY DRESSED IN PINK AND BLUE, BUT SOME SOLDIERS ARE LETTING THEIR SIDE DOWN! CAN YOU FIND THE SOLDIER WHO HAS FORGOTTEN HIS SOCKS AND BOOTS AND 16 SOLDIERS STICKING OUT THEIR TONGUES?

THE GREAT ESCAPE

PHEW, WALDO-FOLLOWERS, I'M HERE IN THIS A-MAZE-ING MAZE, AND I'M NOT THE ONLY ONE! FOUR HOODED TEAMS ARE LOST IN HERE AND CAN'T FIND A WAY OUT! SOME HAVE INVENTED GREAT ESCAPES— BY ROCKET, BY BALLOON, AND BY CATAPULT! THERE IS ONLY ONE WAY THROUGH THIS MAZE— CAN YOU HELP THEM FIND IT?

THE ENORMOUS PARTY

WOW! HOW EXCITING! ARE YOU
IN THE MOOD FOR A PARTY,
WALDO-WATCHERS? LOOK AT THE
BALLOONS, THE STREAMERS, AND
ALL THE SMILING FACES! THE
FLAGS OF 18 COUNTRIES ARE
FLYING HERE — CAN YOU SPOT
SIX FLAGS THAT HAVE SOMETHING
WRONG WITH THEM? *

* THE ANSWERS
ARE IN PART TWO OF
THE CHECKLISTS.
NO CHEATING!